D0090600

A GOLDEN BOOK • NEW YORK

TM & © 2012 The Jim Henson Company. *Triceratops for Lunch* TM & © 2010 The Jim Henson Company. *Hooting, Tooting Dinosaurs* TM & © 2011 The Jim Henson Company. *The Spiky Stegosaurus* TM & © 2012 The Jim Henson Company. JIM HENSON'S mark & logo, DINOSAUR TRAIN mark & logo, characters and elements are trademarks of The Jim Henson Company. All Rights Reserved. The PBS KIDS logo is a registered mark of Public Broadcasting Service (PBS)® 2009. Published in the United States by Golden Books, an imprint of Random House Children's Books, a division of Random House, Inc., 1745 Broadway, New York, NY 10019, and in Canada by Random House of Canada Limited, Toronto. The stories contained in this work were originally published separately by Golden Books as follows: *Triceratops for Lunch,* adapted by Andrea Posner-Sanchez and illustrated by Caleb Meurer, in 2010; *Hooting, Tooting Dinosaurs,* adapted by Andrea Posner-Sanchez and illustrated by Paul Conrad, in 2011; and *The Spiky Stegosaurus,* adapted by Andrea Posner-Sanchez and illustrated by Dave Aikins, in 2012. Golden Books, A Golden Book, A Little Golden Book, the G colophon, and the distinctive gold spine are registered trademarks of Random House, Inc.

randomhouse.com/kids
pbskids.org/dinosaurtrain
ISBN: 978-0-307-931061
MANUFACTURED IN SINGAPORE
10 9 8 7 6 5 4 3 2 1

THE JIM HENSON COMPANY
www.henson.com

Triceratops for Lunch

Buddy, Shiny, Tiny, and Don are heading home to help their mother clean their nest. They are having company!

"Who's coming over?" Buddy asks.

"I don't know," says Tiny, "but I bet they're coming for lunch, and that means we're having fish!"

Like all Pteranodons, Shiny, Tiny, and Don love fish. They eat it all the time. In fact, they even sing a song about it.

"If I could wish
for just one dish,
my greatest wish
would be more

FISH!!!"

Their brother Buddy is a different kind of dinosaur.
He doesn't love fish as much as they do.
"Um . . . does anyone else ever get a little tired
of fish?" he asks.

Tiny, Shiny, and Don can't believe their ears!

Mrs. Pteranodon explains that some dinosaurs don't like fish at all. "Herbivores are dinosaurs that only eat plants," she tells her children. "We are carnivores. We eat meat. Fish is meat."

Later, Mrs. Pteranodon, Buddy, Tiny, and Don go
to the Dinosaur Train Station to meet their guests.
But Don doesn't know what a Triceratops looks like.

TRICERATOPS

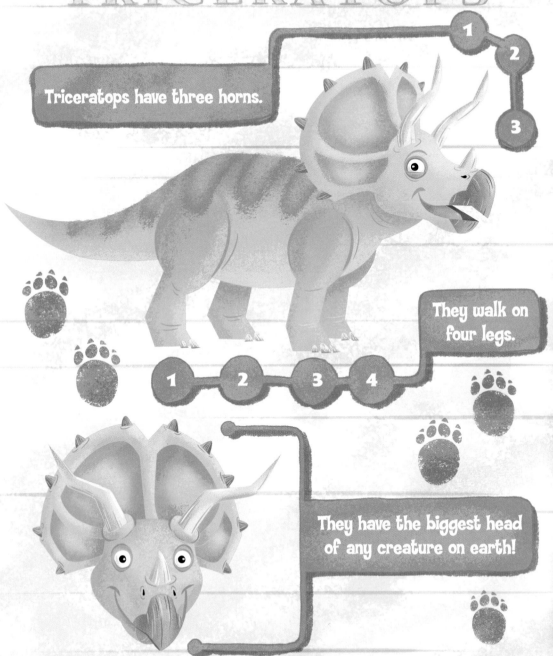

Triceratops have three horns.

1 2 3

They walk on four legs.

1 2 3 4

They have the biggest head of any creature on earth!

"Kids, this is Trudy Triceratops and her son, Tank," Mrs. Pteranodon says as she welcomes her friend.

The kids greet each other.

"High four!"
says Tank.

"High three!"
says Tiny.

"High two!"
adds Buddy
with a laugh.

Don is too amazed by Tank's big
head to join in.

"So, Tank, what sounds more delicious: fish or plants?" Tiny asks.

"Plants!" Tank answers right away. "I'm an herbivore. To me, plants are the best food ever!"

Mrs. Pteranodon is happy to know what to serve her friends for lunch.

But when the two families arrive back at the nest,
it seems Shiny has other plans.
"Ta-daah! Fish!" she announces.

"I don't eat fish," Tank says.

"Fish is your favorite food—you just don't know it yet!" Shiny tells the Triceratops.

Tank is so hungry he agrees to try it.

"Blech!" he declares as he spits the fish out.

Trudy explains that Triceratops' beaks are not made to eat fish. They are perfect for chomping through thick, tough plants.

Tank shows everyone how his beak works by happily eating a whole bush in no time at all.

"Let's ride the Dinosaur Train to the Big Pond," Buddy suggests. "Tank can eat all he wants over there."

On board, Mr. Conductor stops by with the snack cart. He has lots of yummy-looking leafy treats. But Trudy doesn't want Tank to ruin his appetite before lunch.

As soon as they get to the Big Pond, Tank starts eating. He uses his super sharp beak to yank down leaves and chew them up.

"I don't understand," Shiny says. "I have a beak, too, but I don't like leaves at all."

Shiny's beak is long and thin. Tank's beak is short and thick.

Tank has hundreds of teeth. Shiny doesn't have any teeth at all.

Buddy has teeth, too, but they look different from Tank's.

"Maybe *I'm* an herbivore!" Buddy declares. He eats some leaves. They're hard to chew and don't taste very good. "Oh, well, I'll just keep trying new things until I figure out what I like best!"

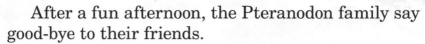

After a fun afternoon, the Pteranodon family say
good-bye to their friends.
"You sure you don't want to try a leafwich? Or a
dipped leaf cluster?" Tank yells to Buddy.
"No leaves for me," Buddy responds. "Bye!"

Back at home, Don pretends to be a Triceratops. "I'll eat all the leaves in the world!" he bellows as he munches on a plant. "Ugh! Leaves taste awful!"

Tiny, Shiny, and Buddy laugh. "Not if you're an herbivore!" says Tiny.

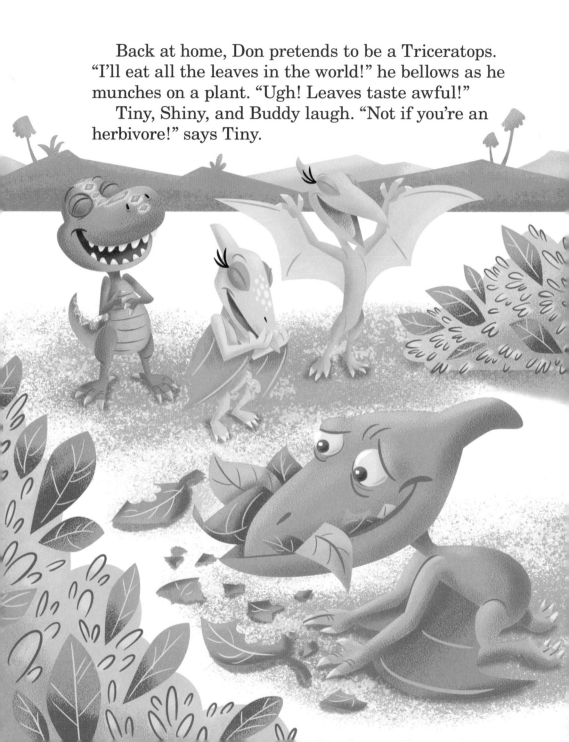

Hooting, Tooting Dinosaurs

One day, Buddy, Shiny, Tiny, and Don were playing outside the nest when their dad walked up to them.

"I've found the perfect birthday present for Mom," said Mr. Pteranodon. "Tickets to a music concert at Corythosaurus Canyon!"

Mr. Pteranodon explained that the Corythosaurus is a dinosaur that makes its own special musical noises.

"I bet they make music with their feet and tails," suggested Shiny.

Everyone went to tell Mom about her birthday gift.
"That's wonderful!" exclaimed Mrs. Pteranodon.

The next morning, the whole family got on the Dinosaur Train. Mr. Conductor collected their tickets. "I see you're heading to a concert," he said. "Be sure to ask a Corythosaurus about its crest."

"What is a crest?" asked Buddy.

Mr. Conductor showed them a picture:

Corythosaurus

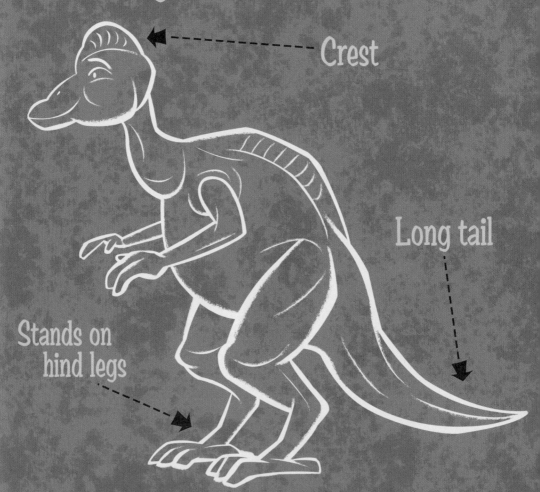

Crest

Long tail

Stands on
hind legs

When the Pteranodon family got off the train, they saw some Corythosaurus heading toward them.

"Hi, we're Mr. and Mrs. Corythosaurus," said the mother dinosaur, "and this is our daughter, Cory."

"Are you here for the concert?" Cory asked.

"We sure are!" responded Mr. Pteranodon.

"Um, Cory? Can we see your crest?" Buddy asked shyly.

Cory bowed her head to show off her crest to her new friends. "Pretty cool, huh?"

Then, while Shiny stayed with the grown-ups, Cory took Buddy, Tiny, and Don on a tour of the canyon. As they walked around, the siblings asked more questions about Cory's crest.

"Do you use it to breathe underwater?"

"Is it a princess crown?"

"Does it have something to do with your Corythosaurus music?"

"Yes, Tiny!" Cory said. "I breathe air in and it travels all around and through my crest. Then it comes out and sounds like . . ."

All of a sudden, they heard hoots coming from a distance. *HOOT!* Cory hooted back.

"Corythosaurus communicate by hooting," Cory explained. "My mom just hooted to tell me that it's almost time for the concert."

"Before we go, let's play hide-and-hoot," Cory suggested. "I'll hide and you have to guess where I am."

Buddy, Tiny, and Don closed their eyes. Cory hid behind a tree. *HOOT!* The kids opened their eyes and ran to the tree. But Cory had already moved to a different spot.

"Hmm. It sounded like she was here!" said Buddy.

HOOT! They ran to a rock.
Cory wasn't there, either.
  Everyone laughed as they
ran around and around,
trying to find Cory.

HOOT!

"That's my mom again," Cory said. "Time to go to the concert."

"Hooray!" cheered Tiny. "I can't wait to hear you play music with your crest, Cory!"

Buddy, Tiny, and Don joined the rest of their
family in front of the stage.
"Gosh, I'm so excited!" said Mrs. Pteranodon.
"Happy birthday, hon!" Mr. Pteranodon told her.

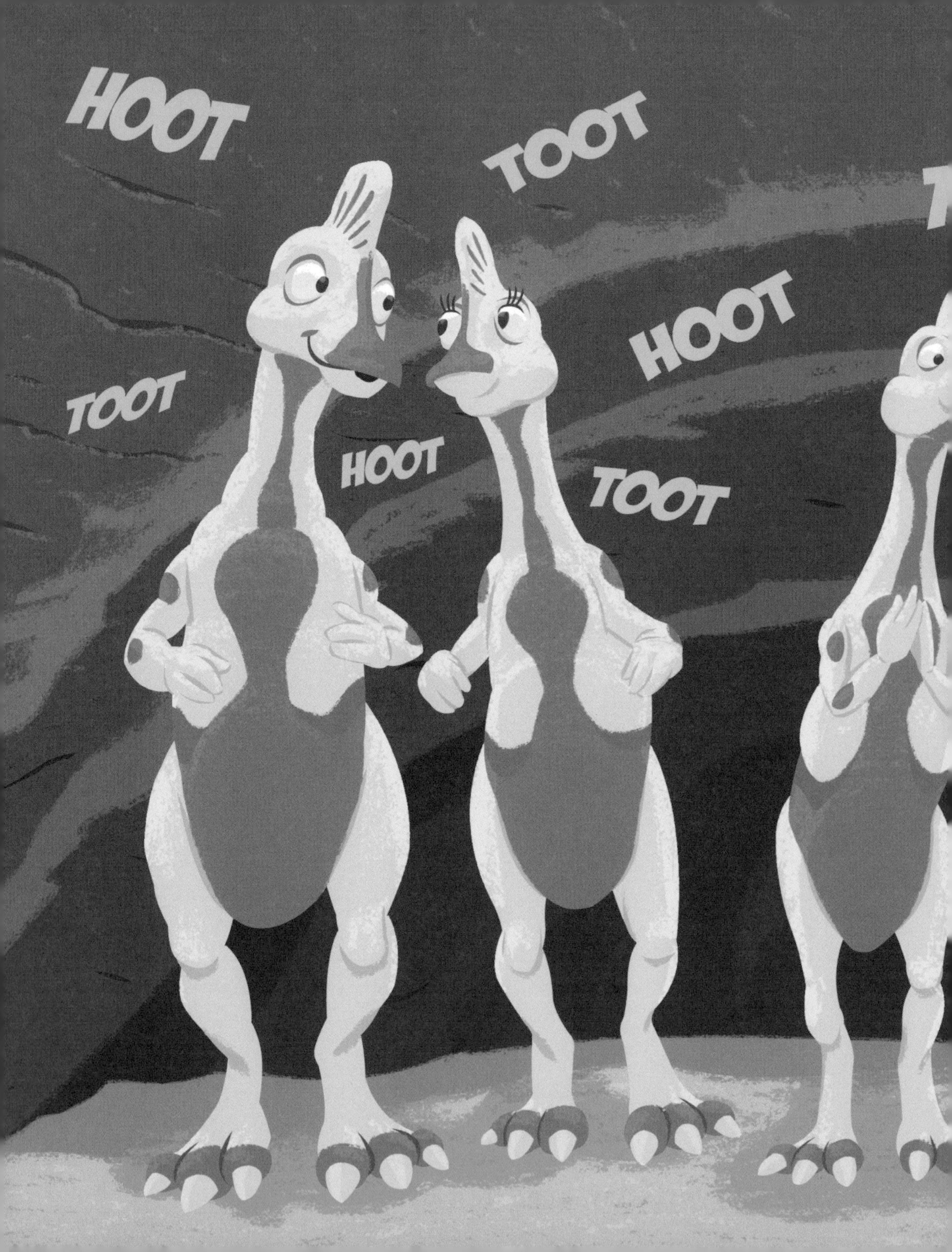
HOOT
TOOT
HOOT
TOOT
HOOT
TOOT

"Welcome to our Corythosaurus concert!" Cory's mom said to the audience. "We are so glad you all are here!"

Then the concert began. All the hooting and tooting sounded great together. And everyone loved Cory's dad's deep hoots.

HOOT

HOOT

TOOT

TOOT

TOOT

"Now it's time for Cory's solo!" Cory's mom announced from the stage.

Little Cory looked nervous. But she made terrific high-pitched hoots all by herself. The Pteranodon family cheered.

When the concert ended, Buddy got an idea. He whispered to his brother and sisters. Then he said, "Mom, we have another present for you."

Buddy, Shiny, and Don hooted as Tiny sang:
"Happy birthday, Mom! Here's your birthday song.
It's really short; it's not too long.
We've got a crest; it's like a flute.
Listen to it hoot and toot!"

The Spiky Stegosaurus

One sunny morning, Tiny and Buddy were taking turns imitating different kinds of dinosaurs. Tiny was pretending to be a Stegosaurus.

"I walk on four legs. I have plates on my back and spikes on my tail," she said. "I use my tail spikes to . . . um . . . carry food around, or . . . um . . . to cool off my body."

Buddy didn't think that sounded right.

Buddy thought of their friend Morris the Stegosaurus. "Morris's spikes go off to the side, not up and down like the plates on his back," he told his sister. "They probably don't cool him."

"They could still catch a breeze!" argued Tiny.

"I don't think they do!" Buddy argued back.

Buddy and Tiny's mom heard the arguing and came right over. She didn't know what Morris Stegosaurus used his spikes for, either.

"Let's visit Morris and ask him," Mrs. Pteranodon suggested.

"Hooray!" shouted Buddy and Tiny.

Mr. Conductor greeted
the Pteranodon family at the
train station. "All aboard the
Dinosaur Train!" he said.

On the train, Mr. Conductor showed Buddy and Tiny a picture of a Stegosaurus.

"See, the spikes stick out to the side," Buddy pointed out.

"But they don't go straight out," insisted Tiny.

Mr. Conductor told them that going to visit Morris was a very smart thing to do. "Asking questions is a great way to find answers."

Soon the train arrived at Stegosaurus Forest.
As Buddy, Tiny, and Mrs. Pteranodon walked
around looking for their friend, they heard voices.
Morris and another dinosaur were arguing. The
Pteranodons rushed toward the sounds.

Morris Stegosaurus and Alvin Allosaurus were standing on opposite sides of a gully. They did not look happy.

"This is my gully, man," said Morris. "And I want to go to that side for the tasty plants."

"Ha! This is *my* gully," Alvin said. "You better stay away from me and let me go to that side to find some good meat to eat."

The two dinosaurs didn't seem to like each other at all.

But once they noticed the Pteranodon family, they smiled and became friendly.

"Awesome to see you guys!" Morris said.

"What are you two arguing about?" asked Buddy.

Morris and Alvin explained that they had never been friends. After all, Allosaurus were predators. They were always trying to catch Stegosaurus.

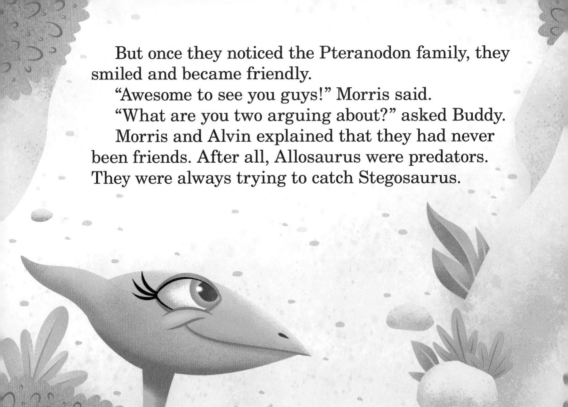

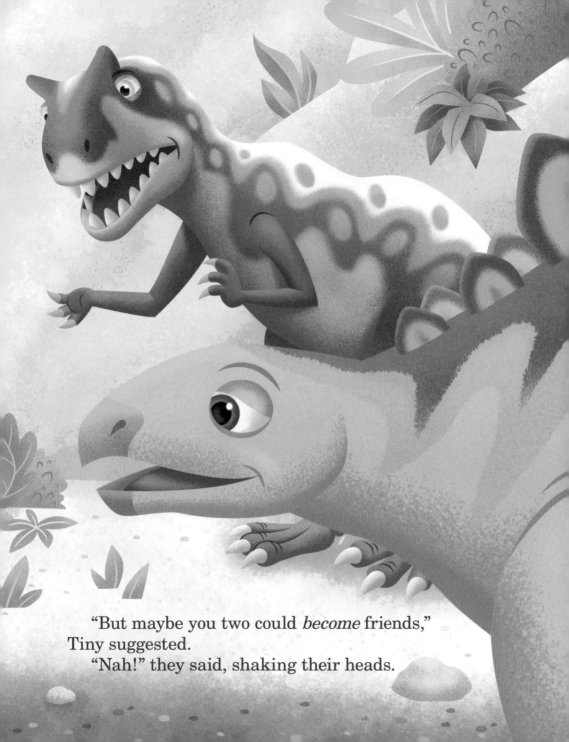

"But maybe you two could *become* friends,"
Tiny suggested.
"Nah!" they said, shaking their heads.

Buddy thought for a second. "Well, we can at least figure out how each of you can get to the other side of the gully without fighting," he said.

"Great idea!" said Mrs. Pteranodon.

Suddenly, Alvin took a step toward the center of the gully.

"Whoa! Stay on your side," Morris yelled as he whipped his tail around.

Alvin jumped away. "Man, that is one dangerous tail!" he said.

Then Buddy and Tiny remembered the reason for their visit.

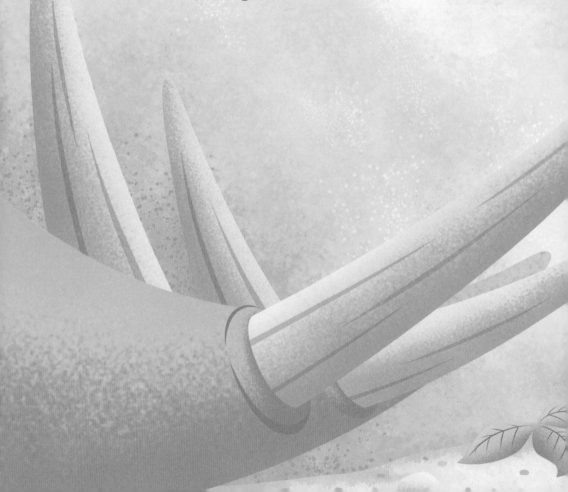

"Morris, Tiny and I were arguing about what you use your spiky tail for," said Buddy.

"Does your spiky tail help you cool down at all?" asked Tiny.

"Naw, the plates on my back do that," Morris answered.

Tiny had another question. "Do you ever carry food on your spikes?"

"I've never carried anything on my spikes. Awesome idea, though," said Morris.

Buddy and Tiny lightly touched
Morris's spikes.

"Very spiky!" they agreed.

"My tail helps me protect myself," explained
Morris. "I'd never hurt you kids with my spiky tail.
But it does keep predators away, if you know what
I mean."

Just then, Morris noticed that Alvin was standing
a little too close for comfort. Morris whipped his spiky
tail around.

"Hey! I was just looking," said Alvin, jumping back.
"I've always been afraid of Morris's spikes, so I avoid
them by moving really fast," he explained to Buddy
and Tiny.

The Pteranodons stepped away for a quick family meeting. "Alvin and Morris are natural enemies. They'll never be best friends," Mrs. Pteranodon told Buddy and Tiny.

"But maybe we can convince them to try to get along," Tiny suggested.

Tiny and Buddy approached the big dinosaurs.
"If you switch sides of the gully, Morris gets his tasty ferns," Tiny said.
"And Alvin gets his meat," continued Buddy. "So do you want to work together and switch?"
Alvin and Morris agreed to give it a try.

Tiny told Alvin and Morris to each take a big step to their right. "Now walk forward."

Buddy reminded both dinosaurs not to swing their tails too much.

"You did it!" shouted Tiny.

"And no one got spiked!" added Buddy.

Alvin and Morris were happy. They even agreed to stop fighting and start being friendly to each other.

Buddy and Tiny realized that they had been fighting, too.

"I'm sorry I argued with you about what Morris's tail spikes were for," Buddy told his sister.

"I'm sorry, too," said Tiny. "I sure know one thing— you're my best friend, Buddy!"